Fairy Tale Fixers
Fixing Fairy Tale Problems with STEM

GOLDILOCKS
AND THE THREE BEARS

Take the Temperature Test and Solve the Porridge Puzzle!

Jasmine Brooke

Gareth Stevens
PUBLISHING

Please visit our website, www.garethstevens.com.
For a free color catalog of all our high-quality books,
call toll free 1-800-542-2595 or fax 1-877-542-2596.

Cataloging-in-Publication Data
Names: Brooke, Jasmine.
Title: Goldilocks and the three bears: take the temperature test and solve the
porridge puzzle! / Jasmine Brooke.
Description: New York : Gareth Stevens Publishing, 2018. | Series: Fairy tale fixers:
fixing fairy tale problems with STEM | Includes index.
Identifiers: ISBN 9781538206805 (pbk.) | ISBN 9781538206737 (library bound) |
ISBN 9781538206652 (6 pack)
Subjects: LCSH: Three bears (Tale)--Adaptation--Juvenile fiction. | Temperature
measurements--Juvenile fiction.
Classification: LCC PZ7.B766 Gol 2018 | DDC [E]--dc23

First Edition

Published in 2018 by
Gareth Stevens Publishing
111 East 14th Street, Suite 349
New York, NY 10003

Copyright © 2018 Gareth Stevens Publishing

Produced for Gareth Stevens by Calcium
Editors: Sarah Eason and Harriet McGregor
Designer: Paul Myerscough
Illustrators: David Pavon and Anita Romeo
Consultant: David Hawksett

Printed in the United States of America

CPSIA compliance information: Batch #CS17GS
For further information contact Gareth Stevens, New York, New York at 1-800-542-2595.

CONTENTS

How to Use This Book

Goldilocks faced lots of fairy tale problems, from porridge that was too hot to chairs that were too small! If only she had used some STEM-thinking to fix her problems. Read the story, try out some fun experiments, and use your STEM skills to figure out innovative ways to fix fairy tale problems! Then look for the STEM solutions on page 30 to see if your experiment conclusions are right.

Once upon a time, in a house in a forest, lived three bears. In this family of bears was a great big father bear, a medium-sized mother bear, and a tiny baby bear.

Every day, the bear family ate a breakfast of delicious, creamy porridge. One morning, as they sat down to their breakfast, they found that their porridge was too hot to eat. So, the bears decided to go for a walk in the forest while their breakfast cooled.

On this very same morning, a little girl named Goldilocks was also walking through the forest. As she came to a clearing, she saw a pretty cottage—the bears' cottage. Goldilocks knocked on the cottage door, but there was no answer. She looked through the window, but could see no one inside. **Curious**, she gently opened the door to the cottage, and called out, "Hello! Is anyone home?" Again, there was no reply. So, Goldilocks pushed open the door and went inside.

As Goldilocks stepped into the cottage, she saw a table with three chairs: one large chair, one medium-sized chair, and one small chair. Then, Goldilocks saw on the table three bowls of porridge: one large bowl, one medium-sized bowl, and one small bowl. Each had a spoon. "Porridge!" Goldilocks sighed, "My favorite!"

Goldilocks was very hungry and the porridge looked so good. She simply could not **resist**! First, she sat in the great big chair, picked up the large spoon, and tried some of the porridge from the big bowl. But the chair was very big and very hard. The spoon was very heavy, too. And, "Ouch!" cried Goldilocks as she put a spoonful of porridge in her mouth—it was far too hot!

Next, Goldilocks tried the medium-sized chair. But this chair was far too soft. Then, she tried the porridge from the medium-sized bowl. "Awful!" cried Goldilocks, as she tasted a spoonful of the porridge. It was far too cold!

Sighing, Goldilocks sat down on the tiny chair. It was just right! Then, she decided to try the last bowl of porridge—the smallest bowl. She picked up the little spoon, took a scoop of porridge, and said, "Delicious!" Goldilocks whispered as she ate the creamy breakfast, "This porridge is not too hot and not too cold—it is just right!" And she ate it all up.

Test Temperature

Father Bear's porridge would have been "just right" too if Goldilocks had used her STEM skills to cool it down!

"Ouch!" cried Goldilocks as she put a spoonful of porridge in her mouth—it was far too hot! "Some cool science will fix this problem!"

You Will Need

• Pan
• 4 ounces (100 g) dry oats
• 1 pint (500 ml) milk
• Three bowls
• Spoon
• Thermometer
• Ice cubes
• Freezer
• Notepad and pen

Help Goldilocks figure out the best way to cool porridge, also known as oatmeal.

1 Ask an adult to help you make enough oatmeal to fill three bowls. To make oatmeal, put the oats and milk in a pan and gently heat on a stove. Stir occasionally. The oatmeal is ready when it is thick and hot.

2 Put an equal amount of oatmeal in each bowl.

3 Use a thermometer to measure the **temperature** of each bowl of oatmeal. Record the temperature. Be sure to place the thermometer in the center of the bowl each time.

4 Put ice cubes in one bowl of oatmeal. Put the second bowl in the freezer. Leave the third bowl at room temperature.

5 Take the temperature of each bowl every 2 minutes. Record the temperatures. Which bowl cools down most quickly? Why do you think this is?

innovate!

In this experiment, we did not stir the oatmeal once it was in the bowls. Repeat the experiment and this time stir the oatmeal each time you take the temperature. Does stirring make the oatmeal cool down more quickly? Why do you think that is? Note your conclusion, and then turn to the STEM Solutions on page 30 to see if you are right.

Satisfied and full of porridge, Goldilocks leaned back in the tiny chair. But Goldilocks was too big and heavy for it. Crack! The delicate chair broke into pieces and collapsed beneath her!

"Goodness!" Goldilocks cried as she fell to the ground, surrounded by the shattered chair.

BUILD a STOOL

Imagine how different the story might have been if Goldilocks had been an **engineer**!

You Will Need
- 19 popsicle sticks
- Glue
- Craft knife or sharp scissors
- Sugar
- Scale
- Small plastic bag
- Notepad and pen

Goldilocks sat down in the smallest chair. But the little chair was very tiny, and Goldilocks was too big and heavy for it. Crack! The wooden chair broke into pieces . . .
Goldilocks: "Goodness! I really should have used my engineering skills and tested how much weight the chair could take before I sat on it!"

Use your STEM skills to test how much weight a stool can take.

1

Line up nine popsicle sticks, as shown. Glue a popsicle stick across each end to make the seat of your stool. Leave to dry.

2

Ask an adult to cut off ¾ inch (2 cm) from each end of four popsicle sticks. These will form your center sections.

14

Glue two popsicle sticks to one of the center sections you made in step 2. Glue a second center section on top. Repeat this process to make two pairs of stool legs. Leave them to dry.

When the glue on the seat and legs is dry, glue the legs to the underside of the seat. You may need to hold them in position or prop them up until the glue is dry.

Use a scale to weigh 0.5 ounce (14 g) of sugar. Put this in your plastic bag. Place it on the stool. Does the stool collapse? If not, keep on adding an extra 0.5 ounce (14 g) of sugar to the bag. How much weight can the stool take before it collapses?

innovate!

How can you strengthen your stool? Where was its weak point? Did the legs collapse or the seat itself? Can it be strengthened by changing the type of glue you use or by adding extra popsicle sticks to the seat or legs? Note your conclusion, and then turn to the STEM Solutions on page 30 to see if you are right.

Brushing the chair splinters from her skirt, Goldilocks decided to explore the cottage. Curious to see what was upstairs, she climbed the winding wooden stairs to the bedroom. Goldilocks pushed open the door and peered into the room. There, she found three wooden beds: one great big bed, one medium-sized bed, and one tiny little bed. "How lovely!" Goldilocks exclaimed. "And I am feeling a little sleepy now."

Yawning, Goldilocks climbed into the great big bed and lay down. She pulled the covers up over her, plumped up the pillows, and curled up to go to sleep. But the big bed was really very big. And the mattress was truly very hard. And Goldilocks was not at all comfortable. She could not get to sleep. "No," Goldilocks said to herself. "This bed will not do."

Next, Goldilocks tried the medium-sized bed. Again, she pulled the covers up over her, plumped up the pillows, and curled up to go to sleep. But the pillows were far too soft. So, too, was the mattress. And Goldilocks just could not get to sleep. "No," she sighed. "This bed will not do either."

Sighing, Goldilocks walked over to the little bed. She climbed into it, plumped up the pillows, and pulled the covers over her. This time the bed was not too big and the mattress was neither too hard nor too soft. In fact, the bed felt just right. "Ah," sighed Goldilocks. "This bed is perfect." And, cozy, warm, and comfortable, she fell fast asleep.

As Goldilocks lay fast asleep in the little bed, the three bears returned from their walk in the forest. Looking forward to their porridge breakfast, they pushed open the door to the cottage and stepped inside. As they did so, they realized that someone had been inside their home.

Father Bear roared with a big, booming voice, "Someone has been sitting in my chair."

Mother Bear said in a quiet, gentle voice, "Someone has been sitting in my chair, too."

Then Baby Bear cried with a squeaky little voice, "Someone has been sitting in my chair, and they have broken it into pieces. Look!"

All three bears looked in horror at Baby Bear's broken little chair, splintered into pieces on the floor. Who could have done such a thing?!

Next, Father Bear looked at his big bowl of porridge and saw the spoon in it. Banging his fist on the table, he cried in his big, booming voice, "Someone has been eating my porridge!"

Mother Bear saw that her medium-sized bowl had a spoon in it. She whispered in her quiet, gentle voice, "Oh, dear. Someone has been eating my porridge, too!"

Then, Baby Bear cried with his squeaky little voice, "Someone has been eating my porridge too, and they have eaten it all up. Look!"

All three bears stared in disbelief at Baby Bear's empty porridge bowl. Who could be so cruel that they would eat a baby's porridge?!

Wondering what kind of a beast they would find, the three bears crept upstairs. **Tentatively**, Father Bear pushed open the door to the bedroom. Mother Bear huddled behind him. Baby Bear huddled behind Mother Bear. Then, Father Bear peeked into the bedroom.

In his big, booming voice, Father Bear cried, "Someone has been sleeping in my bed!"

Mother Bear saw that her bed, too, had the bedclothes turned back and that her pillows were crumpled. She whispered in her quiet, gentle voice, "Somebody has been sleeping in my bed, too!"

Then, Baby Bear looked at his bed. It, too, was crumpled, but, even worse, someone—or something—was beneath the bedclothes. With a gulp, Baby Bear squeaked, "Somebody is sleeping in my bed! And they are still there. Look!"

Baby Bear squeaked so loudly that Goldilocks woke up with a start. As she rubbed her eyes, she saw three furry faces, looking down at her in amazement. "Bears!" cried Goldilocks. "Help!"

Terrified, Goldilocks threw off the bedclothes and leaped from Baby Bear's bed. She hurtled out of the bedroom. She flew down the winding wooden stairs. She raced past the shattered chair on the floor, fled past the porridge bowls, and ran straight through the doorway to the cottage.

Goldilocks ran into the forest clearing and along the forest path. She ran and ran and ran, right through the forest and all the way home.

And the three bears never saw her again!

make a scale model

Would Baby Bear's bed really have been the right size for Goldilocks? Perhaps she should have done the math before trying out the beds!

Sighing, Goldilocks walked over to the little bed. She climbed into it, plumped up the pillows, and pulled the covers over her.
Goldilocks: "Argh, this bed is perfectly awful! Surely there must be a bed that fits me. Let's do the math!"

Help Goldilocks discover which bed would have been the best fit for her.

IMPORTANT INFORMATION:

- An adult male grizzly bear is 8 feet (2.4 m) long.
- An adult female grizzly bear is 6 feet (1.8 m) long.
- A young baby grizzly bear is 2 feet (0.6 m) long.
- A 10-year-old girl is 4.5 feet (1.4 m) tall.

1 Draw a rectangle on a piece of card stock. It should be 8 inches (20 cm) long and 4 inches (10 cm) wide. Cut it out. This is a **scale model** of a bed for Father Bear. We have used 1 inch (2.5 cm) to **represent** 1 foot (30 cm).

2 Draw and cut out another rectangle on card stock to make a bed for Mother Bear. The bed should be 6 inches (15 cm) long and 3 inches (7.5 cm) wide.

3 Draw and cut out another rectangle to make a bed for Baby Bear. It should be 2 inches (5 cm) long and 1 inch (2.5 cm) wide.

4

Put your "Goldilocks" doll in Father Bear's bed. Make sure that Goldilocks's feet are at the bottom of the bed, then use a ruler to measure the distance between the top of her head and the top of the bed. Note the distance. How much smaller is Goldilocks than Father Bear?

5

Put Goldilocks in Mother Bear's bed and then in Baby Bear's bed. Again, each time use a ruler to measure the distance between the top of Goldilocks's head and the top of the bed. How much bigger or smaller is Goldilocks than Mother Bear and Baby Bear? Of all the beds, which bed is the best fit? Can you find the difference in height between Goldilocks and the combined height of the bears? Use this equation to help you:

$$8 \text{ feet} + 6 \text{ feet} + 2 \text{ feet} - 4.5 \text{ feet} = ? \text{ feet}$$

Innovate!

If the bears all wanted to sleep in the same bed at the same time, how big would it have to be? Use the measurements for length and width that you used in this experiment to create a model of the bed. How long and how wide should it be? Turn to the STEM Solutions on page 30 to see if you are right.

STEM SOLUTIONS

Test Temperature

The oatmeal in the freezer cooled most quickly. The air in the freezer is much colder than air at room temperature and also colder than the ice cubes. **Heat energy** moved very quickly from the oatmeal into the air.

Stirring caused the oatmeal to cool more quickly, too. When you stir oatmeal, the warmer oatmeal beneath the cooler surface oatmeal is moved to the top of the bowl. It is exposed to the air and cooled. Stirring in the ice cubes moved them through the warm oatmeal beneath the surface, cooling the oatmeal more quickly.

Build a Stool

The weakest place in the stool was the point at which the underside of the seat met the crossbar at the top of the legs. To strengthen the stool and allow it to hold more weight, you could have used stronger glue or increased the number of legs on the underside of your stool.

Make a Scale Model

Goldilocks is 3.5 feet (1 m) shorter than Father Bear, 1.5 feet (46 cm) shorter than Mother Bear, and 2.5 feet (72 cm) taller than Baby Bear. Goldilocks is 11.5 feet (3.5 m) shorter than the combined height of all three bears. Mother Bear's bed is the best fit for Goldilocks. A bed big enough for all three bears would be 8 feet (2.4 m) long and 8 feet (2.4 m) wide.

FURTHER READING

Books

Amazing Visual Math. New York, NY: DK Children, 2014.

Braun, Eric. *Goldilocks and the Three Bears: An Interactive Fairy Tale Adventure* (You Choose: Fractured Fairy Tales). Minneapolis, MN: Capstone Press, 2015.

Ceceri, Kathy. *Robotics: Discover the Science and Technology of the Future with 20 Projects* (Build It Yourself). White River Junction, VT: Nomad Press, 2012.

Heineck, Liz Lee. *Kitchen Science Lab for Kids: 52 Family Friendly Experiments from Around the House* (Lab). Beverly, MA: Quarry Books, 2014.

Websites

Discover the answers to all your science questions at:
askdruniverse.wsu.edu

Apply your STEM skills and knowledge at:
pbskids.org/zoom/activities/sci

Get excited about engineering at:
www.egfi-k12.org

Try out lots of fun activities at:
www.exploratorium.edu/explore

GLOSSARY

curious very interested in something

engineer a person who uses engineering skills to make things and find solutions to problems

heat energy the amount of heat in something

model a recreation of an object, usually in smaller form, to show how it looks and functions

represent to show or describe something

resist to stop or try to stop something

scale the relation between the real size of something and its size on a model

temperature the measurement of how hot or cold something is

tentatively very carefully and nervously

INDEX